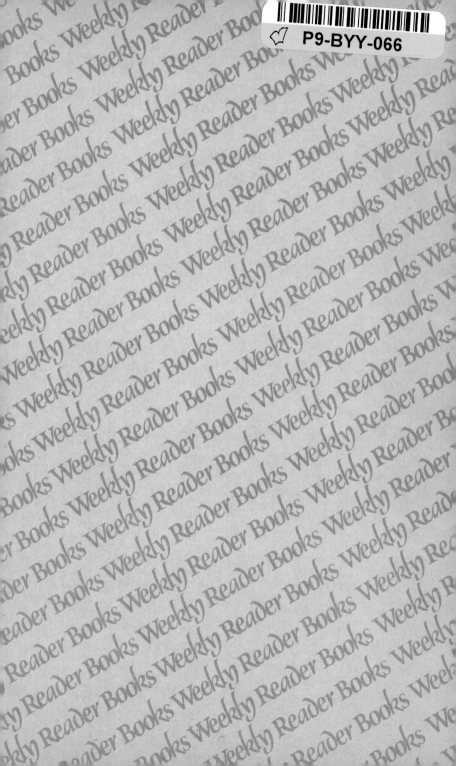

❦ BOOK REVIEW

Mrs. Rashoon is very different from Stella's third grade teacher, Mrs. Mazursky, who Stella thought was perfect. Then a softball tournament, in which Stella's class plays against Mrs. Mazursky's third grade, teaches Stella a few things about her favorite teacher, about perfection and about herself, making for both a funny and perceptive story.

from L E A R N I N G

Weekly Reader Books presents

Not Even Mrs. Mazursky

by Jane Sutton

illustrated by Joan Drescher

E. P. DUTTON · NEW YORK

This book is a presentation of Weekly Reader Books.
Weekly Reader Books offers book clubs for children
from preschool through high school. For further
information write to: **Weekly Reader Books,**
4343 Equity Drive, Columbus, Ohio 43228.

Edited for Weekly Reader Books and published by
arrangement with E.P. Dutton, Inc.

Library of Congress Cataloging in Publication Data

Sutton, Jane.
  Not even Mrs. Mazursky.

  Summary: Stella's "fantastic" teacher from last year
lets her down in a very disappointing way and she must
come to grips with the realization that no one is perfect.
  [1. Schools—Fiction.] I. Drescher, Joan E., ill.
II. Title.
PZ7.S96824No 1984 [Fic] 83-20678
ISBN 0-525-44083-6

Published in the United States by E. P. Dutton, Inc.,
2 Park Avenue, New York, N. Y. 10016

Editor: Ann Durell   Designer: Claire Counihan

Printed in the U.S.A.

to Judy,
my big sister,
for never getting tired of giving

Not Even
Mrs. Mazursky

Chapter 1

My name is Stella Nash, and I want to talk about teachers. Some of them are terrific. But some are_____(you can fill in the blank with a not-so-nice word).

Last year I was in third grade, and I had a fantastic teacher named Mrs. Mazursky. She's just about perfect.

This year, my teacher is Mrs. Rashoon. She's perfect too—perfectly awful. Mrs. Rashoon never smiles. And she gives us too much work. When I talk about her to my friends, I just call her Rashoon—I leave out the Mrs. Calling someone Mr.

or Miss or Mrs. is a way to show respect. And I have no respect for Rashoon.

If you say one word in class when you're supposed to be working, Rashoon stares at you with a look that could break someone's glasses, kill a dragon, and make milk go sour (well, maybe I'm exaggerating a little). Then she says, "I don't mind if *you* don't want to work, Stella, but you're disturbing your neighbors. Anyone who doesn't want to work may go sit at the blue table in the back of the classroom."

Rashoon even looks horrible. She has black, painted-on eyebrows that make her look as mean as she is.

Mrs. Mazursky would never act like Rashoon. Let's say I was fooling around during a work time. Mrs. Mazursky would say, "Ahem! Ahem! Your mind is wandering, Stella. It was just spotted at the gymnasium." Everybody would laugh, and I would get back to work.

When I grow up, I want to be like Mrs. Mazursky. She's friendly and funny and smart and nice. She has a great singing voice, and she can play the piano really well.

Mrs. Mazursky always gave us assignments that were fun. For example, we played an indoor baseball game where you would get "hits" and "runs" if you knew the multiplication tables.

Another time, she had us write a poem about what we would like to change about school. My poem went like this:

4

What I Would Change About School

If it were up to me,
   school would be more free,
   you could always climb a tree.
You wouldn't have to spell
   or wait for any bells,
   I'd leave in show 'n' tell.
There would be *no* multiplication
   or boring information,
   and we'd have many more vacations!

My mother still has my poem taped to our refrigerator.

Rashoon wouldn't *think* of having fun in school. Actually, her idea of fun is being mean to kids. My friend Rachel says people like Rashoon shouldn't be allowed to be teachers. My friend Debbie says Rashoon must be friends with the principal. Otherwise, she would have been fired a long time ago for being too mean.

It's hard to be friends with both Debbie and Rachel, even though we're all in the same class. They don't like each other very much. In fact, they hate each other. I can never invite them both to my house at the same time. I can't even talk to them on the playground at the same time.

Debbie says Rachel is a creep, because Rachel has long, frizzy hair that sticks out in a big triangle, and all she does is read, or write poetry, even during recess. Sometimes Rachel wears the same outfit three days in a row.

5

Rachel says Debbie is stuck-up, because Debbie won't even talk to kids she thinks are creeps, and because she's always telling everyone how rich her parents are. Her parents are about the richest people in Crafton, which is where we live. Her father owns a chain of sporting goods stores.

Everyone wants to be Debbie's friend because she never acts afraid, and she comes up with neat games to play during recess. Also, you never know when Debbie might decide you're a creep and drop you, so it's kind of exciting to be her friend.

Even though Debbie is a little stuck-up and Rachel is a little creepy, I like both of them. But they sure are different. The only thing they agree about is that Rashoon is for the birds.

You should see what happens when Rashoon is sick and our class has a substitute. We go WILD!

Last Tuesday, there was no Rashoon when the bell rang at nine o'clock.

"Maybe she's sick," Ronnie Brazelton said.

"I'll say she's sick," said Kevin Landers. "But that never stopped her from coming to school before."

Just then, a thin lady with long black hair and glasses on the end of her nose came in. She looked young.

"Good morning, boys and girls," she said. "My name is Miss Simpson. Mrs. Rashoon will not be in today, and I will be your substitute."

"All right!" half the class said.

6

"Yay!" said the other half.

Miss Simpson looked kind of nervous. You could tell she hadn't done much substituting before.

Right away, kids started taking advantage of her. "Can I go to the bathroom?" asked Ronnie.

"Let's take attendance first," said Miss Simpson.

"I *really* have to go to the bathroom," said Ronnie.

"OK," said Miss Simpson, looking embarrassed. "What's your name, so I can mark you on the list?"

"Michael Brown," said Ronnie on his way out the door.

Everyone laughed, especially Michael Brown.

Miss Simpson took attendance, and we all answered to each others' names. When she said "Susan Thomas," who was on vacation with her parents, someone shouted, "She died."

"Oh, I'm really sorry," said Miss Simpson. "No one told me."

I felt sorry for Miss Simpson because our class was giving her a hard time. But we couldn't help it. Having Rashoon absent felt as if we were allowed out of jail for the day.

"Mrs. Rashoon has given me her lesson plans," said Miss Simpson when she finished taking attendance. "Please take out your mathematics workbooks and start on page 23."

Johnny Surbeck got up and lay down on the floor in the back of the classroom.

"Excuse me, young man, what are you doing?" asked Miss Simpson.

"I'm very tired. I need to lie down," said Johnny.

"Why are you so tired?" asked Miss Simpson. She looked at him over the top of her glasses that she wore at the end of her nose. "What's your name?"

"Fred Williams," said Johnny.

"I don't seem to find that name on the list," said Miss Simpson.

"Miss Simpson?" said Sally Andrews.

"Yes?" answered Miss Simpson.

"Well, Fred doesn't like to talk about it," said Sally in a loud whisper, "but his parents are alcoholics. He doesn't get much sleep at home. You know, with all the shouting and fighting."

"Oh," said Miss Simpson sadly. "Does Mrs. Rashoon let him sleep in class?"

"Oh yes," about six kids said, including Ronnie Brazelton, who was just coming back from the bathroom.

At nine thirty, my friend Debbie said, "Time for recess, everyone!"

"Recess?" asked Miss Simpson.

"Yes, at nine thirty," I said. "The bell hasn't been working lately." I thought Debbie would be pleased with me for going along with her joke.

8

We all closed our workbooks and ran, laughing, into the hall. Johnny Surbeck woke up from his "sleep" in the back of the classroom and was one of the first out the door.

The principal, Dr. Rogers, heard the commotion. She marched up to us and sent us back to our classroom.

After a short talk with Dr. Rogers, Miss Simpson told us to get back to work. She looked as if she had aged ten years in the forty-five minutes she had been substituting in our classroom.

We settled down to work for a while. Then a whisper started to go around the classroom. "At ten thirty, everybody with glasses . . . put them on the end of your nose, like Miss Simpson. Everybody else, make a pair of pipe cleaner eyeglasses."

We had pipe cleaners left over from an art project in our desks. Everyone got busy making pipe cleaner eyeglasses while pretending to work on multiplication problems in our workbooks. At ten thirty, we put on our eyeglasses, being sure to wear them on the ends of our noses, like our poor substitute teacher.

Lucy Talbot, wearing a bright pink pair of pipe cleaner eyeglasses, raised her hand and asked, "Miss Simpson, will Mrs. Rashoon be here tomorrow?"

"Well, I'm not sure," began Miss Simpson. Then she looked around and saw everyone wearing pipe cleaner or real eyeglasses on the ends of their

noses. Her face turned red. You could tell she didn't know what to say.

Finally, she said, "You may work quietly on whatever you like until lunchtime."

Lunchtime was almost an hour away. We raced around the classroom and made lots of noise. Kids chewed gum and put their feet up on desks.

Miss Simpson didn't seem to care anymore. She sat at her desk and read a book.

After our lunch recess, we had a new substitute. Mr. Saruto, the gym teacher, took over the class. He told us Miss Simpson had a doctor's appointment. We all giggled and winked at each other.

We didn't try anything smart with Mr. Saruto, because he's a regular teacher and we have to see him twice a week in gym class.

I wondered what Miss Simpson was doing. I felt sorry for her. She would be surprised to see how well-behaved our class was with Mr. Saruto and with mean old Rashoon.

If only we had Mrs. Mazursky again this year, I thought.

Chapter 2

At dinner that night, I told my family about the trouble our class gave Miss Simpson.

When I got to the part about wearing pipe cleaner eyeglasses, my mother said, "You kids are terrible!" But I could tell she was trying not to laugh.

My brother, Tom, who is seventeen, said, "Oh, Mom, what Stella's class did was nothing! You should see what goes on in high school." Tom thinks everything I do is just kid stuff.

"Tom's fellow students are so tough that they

need *three* substitutes for each class," said my father.

My mother and I laughed.

"Very funny, Dad," said Tom.

My sister, Tanya, who had just turned a year and a half, didn't say anything about Miss Simpson. Maybe she did, but I didn't understand it. She said, "Da dada da mee mee nee." I wish there were a dictionary that told what baby words mean. That way, I would know what Tanya is talking about.

"Hey, Mom, I'd like to talk about something more important," said Tom. "How come we've had chicken every night this week?"

I hadn't noticed it, but Tom was right. That night, we had broiled chicken. The night before, we had had chicken tetrazzini. And the night before that, we had had roast chicken.

"Chicken was on sale," muttered my mother. "At 59¢ a pound, how could I pass up buying a few?"

"It figures," said Tom.

"You and your sales, Mammu," I said. I don't know how I got started calling my mother Mammu. I think I just wanted to call her something different from Mom or Mommy.

"Exactly how many chickens did you buy?" asked my father.

"Oh, six, maybe seven," said my mother sheepishly.

You know how people do all sorts of things to make themselves feel good? Well, my mother buys things on sale. She *loves* to buy things on sale. She *has* to buy things on sale.

She claims that she saves lots of money finding bargains. My father says she doesn't really save money because she spends so much on gas, driving to different stores to find the cheapest prices. She buys her bread at the Crafton Bakery. She buys meat at Bill's Foodmaster. She buys canned goods at Wolfersteins. The stores are all in different parts of Crafton. So I think my father is right about her spending a lot on gas.

Also, lots of times, my mother buys things that we don't need, just because they're on sale. Once, we had a whole freezer full of sausages that were marked 20 percent off. Everyone in my family hates sausages. But my mother got so excited when she saw how cheap they were that she forgot everyone hates them, and she bought fifteen packages of sausages.

My father doesn't usually get angry. But sometimes my mother's sale "thing" really burns him up. He tells her she must be bored to spend so much time cutting out coupons and running from store to store to save twenty cents. He says she ought to go back to work.

My mother used to be a kindergarten teacher, but she quit after I was born. She says she would rather stay home and take care of us kids than work. Besides, she says that even if she wanted to go back to work, there aren't enough jobs for kindergarten teachers.

"Can we have hamburgers instead of chicken for dinner tomorrow?" asked Tom.

"OK," said my mother. "I think Bill's Foodmaster is having a special on chopped meat anyway."

"How about French fries too?" I asked. French fries are about my favorite food in the world.

"Hamburgers and French fries, it will be," said my mother.

"Da dee dee da nee," said Tanya, banging her spoon on her high chair tray.

"You're right, Tanya," I said. She grinned at me, showing off her little white teeth.

The phone rang.

"Hi hi," said Tanya. That's what she always says when the phone rings.

My father answered the phone. "Nash residence," he said in a phony English accent. "Whoever you are, I hope this is important. You've interrupted our dinner. . . ."

There was a pause and then he said, "No, that's OK, I was just kidding. . . . Yes, he's right here, Roberta. . . ."

Tom started to get up from his chair and my father said, "It's for you, Romeo."

Tom frowned and said, "Very funny, Dad. . . . It's Roberta?"

"Sure sounds like her," said my father.

Our phone has a long extension cord, so Tom brought it out into the living room to talk.

"Did you say that was Roberta?" I asked, surprised.

"Isn't that his girlfriend's name?" asked my father.

"No, it's Cheryl!" said my mother. "He broke up with Roberta weeks ago."

"I guess that's why she didn't say anything after I called her Roberta," my father said sheepishly.

"When they passed out memories, they forgot to give you one," said my mother. "Why don't you pay attention to what goes on here?"

My father, as you may have guessed, is kind of absentminded. He's always leaving his keys in his car or taking someone else's shopping cart by mistake. If he gets up to buy popcorn in the movies, he forgets where he was sitting. If my mother asks him to go to the drug store and buy a newspaper, he comes home with toothpaste.

Sometimes trying to get my father's attention is like standing on the ground and waving to people in an airplane. They just can't see you.

You can be in the middle of telling him something, when you notice that his eyes are staring into space. Just staring. It can be annoying.

Most of the time, my father is thinking about the latest speech he's working on. He has his own business, writing for people who have to give speeches and don't know what to say. He might write a speech for the president of a company or for a candidate for mayor. He has an office right in our house. It has its own entrance, or you can get to it by walking through our living room.

Sometimes he has to think of jokes to put in the speeches, so no one in the audience will fall asleep. He has a fine sense of humor, so he's good at it. If you're in the middle of telling my father something serious and he starts laughing, it's usually because he just thought of a joke to use in a speech.

It would be hard for *anyone* to remember the name of Tom's girlfriend. Tom changes girlfriends every month. He's very cute and smart, and he's an excellent athlete and a good drummer. So he has no trouble finding girlfriends. Just when you think he's going to settle down with one of his girlfriends for a while, he's going out with someone new.

When Tom got off the phone, my father said, "Please apologize to Cheryl for me the next time you see her. I called her Roberta by mistake."

"That was Anita!" said Tom. "Cheryl is history, Dad. I haven't seen her in over a week."

My parents and I burst out laughing. Tanya started laughing too. She thinks it's funny when people laugh.

"I wonder if I could use this situation in a speech," said my father, jotting down notes on his paper napkin.

"No one would believe it," I said.

Chapter 3

The next day in school, Debbie came over to me with a gleam in her eye. I knew she was up to something. She showed me a note she had found that said "I hate Debbie."

We could tell right away from the sloppy handwriting that the note was written by Elsie Hoover. Elsie is a creep. She's so tall that she walks with her head bent forward like a llama. She has terrible taste in clothing—she might wear a plaid skirt and a checked blouse. Whenever Rashoon asks a question, Elsie raises her hand and says, "I know! I know!" Usually, her answer is wrong, and she blushes redder than anyone I've ever seen.

Most of the time, I don't mind Elsie. I feel sorry for her. But she really bugs me when she steals jokes. I might say something funny to a kid sitting next to me. Elsie will repeat it loudly, hoping the rest of the class will think it was her joke.

Anyway, most people who found a note that said someone hated them would throw it out or hide it or burn it or at least feel bad that someone hated them. Not Debbie. I guess she thinks no one has a right to hate her.

Debbie told me she wanted me to help her blackmail Elsie. Blackmail is when you threaten someone that you'll tell people bad things about them if they don't give you money. Debbie learned about blackmail from watching "Ed Crocker, Private Eye," her favorite TV show. Debbie has her own TV, right in her room.

"But how can you blackmail Elsie?" I asked Debbie. "She doesn't have much money."

"I don't want money," said Debbie. "My parents buy me just about anything I want."

"Well, what *do* you want?" I asked.

"Tootsie Rolls!" said Debbie. "I love Tootsie Rolls. But whenever I ask for them, my mother says they're too fattening and they're bad for my teeth. Elsie's parents own a candy store, so it will be easy for her to get them."

"I still don't understand what you can threaten her with," I said.

"Sometimes you're really thick," said Debbie.

"We'll just tell her that if she won't give me two Tootsie Rolls every day, I'll show the whole class the note she wrote about me. I know she'll go along with it."

Debbie was right. Elsie wouldn't want anyone to find out she hated Debbie. Debbie was so popular that if people found out Elsie hated her, they would hate *Elsie*. And she was a creep as it was.

Debbie's plan reminded me of the time she got me to help her hide her big brother's homework. The poor guy was searching everywhere for it, until I finally told him it was hidden inside the cover of a Beatles album.

"I don't know if I want to blackmail Elsie with you," I said. "Rachel says she has 'soul.'"

"Don't you be a creep too, like Rachel and Elsie," said Debbie. She stamped her feet angrily, making her blonde curls bounce. "All you have to do is come with me and agree with everything I say. We can dress up like the big-time criminals on 'Ed Crocker, Private Eye.'"

I didn't want Debbie to drop me and tell everyone I was a creep, which is what she did with all her other friends she dropped. Debbie and I were friends in Mrs. Mazursky's class, right into Rashoon's, which is over a year. That's probably the longest she's ever kept a friend.

I'm not pretty or fearless or rich, and I'm a little shy. So I didn't know how popular I would be if I weren't Debbie's friend. I could already picture her telling everyone I was creepy because I wear my hair in braids.

Anyway, it did sound kind of fun to pretend I was a big-time criminal. So I agreed to go along with Debbie's blackmail plan. . . .

You should have seen Debbie and me during recess the next day! Debbie was wearing her big brother's leather jacket, and she was carrying a motorcycle chain. She wore a black headband that pushed down her hair. I was wearing sunglasses and a black raincoat Debbie had brought to school for me.

We walked up to Elsie, who was shooting baskets by herself. "Elsie baby, we want a word with you," said Debbie in a hoarse, gangster voice.

Elsie looked nervous. She dropped the basketball and followed us to the empty softball field.

"You see this note?" asked Debbie. She showed Elsie the note that said "I hate Debbie."

"Uh huh," said Elsie, blushing as usual.

"You wrote it, didn't you?" asked Debbie.

"Well . . ." said Elsie, turning even redder.

"Don't lie to us," said Debbie.

"OK . . . I wrote it," said Elsie. "I'm sorry, Debbie."

"Sorry doesn't help," said Debbie, sounding really tough. "Does it, Stella?" She poked me in the side with her elbow.

"No, sorry doesn't help," I said.

"Now you wouldn't want anyone to find out you wrote this note, would you?" asked Debbie. She poked me again.

"Would you?" I asked.

"No," said Elsie.

"Well, I won't tell anyone about it," said Debbie.

"Oh, thank you," said Elsie.

"If," said Debbie, "you bring me two Tootsie Rolls every day. Right, Stell?"

"Every day," I said.

"What kind of candy do you want her to bring for you?" Debbie asked me.

"Oh, that's all right, I don't want any," I said.

Debbie gave me a dirty look, and then she said, "You're getting off easy, Elsie. Two Tootsie Rolls every day, and nobody will see this note." She folded it up and put it in the pocket of her motorcycle jacket.

"Can I go now?" asked Elsie.

"Yes, but don't let me down," warned Debbie in her hoarse, criminal voice.

Elsie hurried off with her head way in front of her body.

"We were just like gangsters on 'Ed Crocker,' " said Debbie. "Slap me five!" She held her palm out to me.

I slapped her five, but I wasn't very enthusiastic. I felt sorry for Elsie.

Debbie guessed what I was feeling. "Oh, don't

be a creep and go feeling sorry for *that* creep," she said with disgust.

Sometimes I wondered if it was worth being friends with Debbie. People figured I was OK because I was friends with her. And she came up with lots of wild ideas for things to do. But I didn't always agree with what she did. And now she had gotten me to do something I felt really crummy about.

Chapter 4

The next day in school, I had trouble keeping my mind on multiplication problems. I wanted to talk Debbie out of blackmailing Elsie.

I turned to Debbie, who was sitting next to me, and said, "I don't think it's right for you to . . ."

"Stella, get back to work," said Rashoon.

Yes, Rashoon was back. The illness that brought us Miss Simpson for a substitute had lasted only a day.

Rashoon gave me her usual speech: "I don't mind if *you* don't want to work, Stella, but you're disturbing your neighbors. If you don't want to work, you may go sit at the blue table in the back of the classroom."

Well, I didn't want to work. I was sick of multiplication work sheets and workbooks. I was sick of Rashoon talking about the blue table in the back of the classroom and about not disturbing my neighbors.

So I did something I had thought of before, but never had the nerve to do. I stood up and started walking to the back of the classroom. Halfway there, my heart started pounding. I could feel the whole class staring at me. I decided it was too late to turn back.

I kept walking and then sat down at the table. I stared out the window. Slowly, Rashoon looked up from papers she was correcting, raised her painted-on eyebrows and demanded, "What do you think you're doing, Stella?"

"Well, you said if we didn't want to work, we could sit at this table," I said. I tried not to sound as if my body was shaking like a washing machine in the spin cycle, which it was.

"I never said that," said Rashoon in an even, quiet voice.

I couldn't believe it. Rashoon was telling a real whopper. She must have given her sit-at-the-table-in-back-of-the-classroom-just-don't-disturb-your-neighbors speech three times a day since school started.

"I think you owe the class an apology," said

Rashoon. "You have disturbed everyone who is trying to work."

It was bad enough that she was telling a big, fat lie that everyone knew she was telling. But now she wanted *me* to tell a lie too—she wanted me to say I was sorry for doing something she had said was OK to do in the first place.

I didn't know what to say. I wished I were sick at home, watching TV and sipping some soup my mother bought on sale.

"Stella, I will give you a choice," said Rashoon. She seemed to raise her painted-on eyebrows another three inches. "Either you apologize to the class or you spend the rest of the day in the hall."

There was a lot of whispering going on. I kept sitting at the table without saying anything. I had never been kicked out of class before. But I didn't want to say I was sorry just to keep from getting kicked out.

"What will it be, Stella?" asked Rashoon. "Are you going to apologize?"

"No," I said. "I didn't do anything to apologize for."

Rashoon's black, painted-on eyebrows seemed to go up still another three inches. I thought they would disappear right into her hair. I heard gasps and giggles, "You're in trouble now," "Right on, Stella!" and "Whooooo!" from the other kids.

"That's enough, class!" barked Rashoon. "Stella, leave the classroom, and don't come back until you're ready to apologize!"

As soon as I walked into the empty hall, my stomach felt sick. A voice started chattering inside my head. "Kicked out of class, kicked out of class," it said.

I knew I was right and Rashoon was wrong. But who would believe me if they saw me hanging around the hall? Dr. Rogers, the principal, would probably hate me for being kicked out of class. My parents would be disappointed in me. I wasn't sure what the other kids would think either. Debbie broke plenty of school rules, but she never did anything dumb enough to get kicked out of class.

I thought of asking Mrs. Mazursky if I could stay in her classroom. But I was afraid she would hate me too. Even she would figure I must have done something wrong to get kicked out of class.

I wandered into the girls' bathroom and looked in the mirror. *This is the face of someone who's been kicked out of class,* I thought. I felt more like a gangster than when I dressed up to "blackmail" Elsie.

The swinging door of the girls' room squeaked, and Rachel came in. I was never happier to see that frizzy triangular head of hair.

"How're you doing?" she asked.

"OK, I guess," I said. Then I almost started to cry, and I said, "I don't know what to do. I can't hang around in here all day, but I don't want to apologize to that witch."

"Maybe you could call your mother and ask her

to talk to Rashoon for you," suggested Rachel.

"Do you think my mother would take my side against a teacher?" I asked.

"Sure," said Rachel.

"I guess so," I said. "But the pay phone is right between the principal's office and the teachers' room. Some teacher would see me and ask what I was doing out of class."

"Hmm," said Rachel. "Listen, I have to run. Rashoon guessed that I wanted to talk to you. But I said I really had to go to the bathroom, and I'd just be gone a minute."

"OK, Rach," I said. "Thanks for coming."

"Good luck," said Rachel, and she raced out, her triangle of Brillo hair bobbing up and down as she ran. It was strange to see Rachel run. She doesn't play sports, and she's usually sitting quietly, reading a book or writing poetry. Even though I was miserable, I felt lucky to have such a good friend. Maybe Rachel wasn't as "with it" as Debbie, but she was sure "with me" when I needed her.

Debbie would probably drop me like a hot chili dog if I got into a lot of trouble for being kicked out of class.

I went back into the hall. I thought of leaving school and either hitchhiking home or walking until I found a pay phone to call my mother. Then I remembered it was February in Massachusetts, and it was about 15 degrees outside. My all-weather parka, which my mother bought on sale at Bermans Department Store, was in my locker in the back of the classroom.

As I was bending down to drink from the water fountain, someone tapped my shoulder. It was Michael Brown. "Hi Stell," he said. "I came out to see how you're doing."

"Thanks," I said. "I'm not crazy about hanging around the hall. But I'm OK."

"It took guts for you to get up and walk to that table," he said. "Well, I have to go."

I thought it was nice of Michael to come out to see me. Maybe the other kids in my class wouldn't hate me for getting kicked out either.

I didn't know what to do next. It was getting near lunchtime, and I was hungry. The only way I could join my class for lunch was to apologize. Apologize! *Rashoon* should apologize to the class for lying! It wasn't right that a teacher should lie and be so mean. If only I had Mrs. Mazursky again.

Ronnie Brazelton popped out of our classroom door. "Hey, Stella, are you coming back in or what?" he asked.

"I don't know," I said.

"It's almost time for lunch," he said.

"Ronnie!" barked Rashoon, suddenly behind him. "I thought you wanted a drink of water. I didn't allow you into the hall to talk to people who misbehave!"

She gave me an icy look and said to Ronnie, "I will never trust you again."

Ronnie looked sheepish and started back to the classroom. I HATED Rashoon. She made me feel like a criminal. No one was supposed to even talk to me.

I listened outside the classroom door, and I could hear Rashoon tell the class to line up for lunch. I decided I couldn't wander around the hall all day. So I went back in, hoping I could get in the lunch line, and no one would notice me.

"Stella!" said Rashoon with a satisfied grin when she saw me. "Are you joining us for lunch?"

"Yes," I said.

"First, you will have to apologize to the class for disturbing us," the witch said.

The classroom was totally quiet.

"I apologize," I said.

"For what?" asked Rashoon.

"For disturbing the class," I mumbled. I kept my fingers crossed behind my back, so it wouldn't be such a bad lie.

"I couldn't hear you," she said.

"For disturbing the class," I repeated louder.

"Could we have the whole apology loud enough for everyone to hear this time?" asked Rashoon, grinning.

"I apologize for disturbing the class," I said, loud and clear.

"Fine," said Rashoon. "I assume this won't happen again."

I got on the end of the lunch line. Rachel left her place at the beginning of the line and stood behind me. The lunch bell rang, and Rashoon opened the door. We were let out of jail for fifty minutes.

"Don't feel bad, Stell," whispered Rachel. "There was nothing else you could do."

Chapter 5

After school, I still felt horrible about getting kicked out of class and having to lie to get back in. I went to see Mrs. Mazursky. I visited her lots of times after school, because I liked her so much. We would talk about what I was learning in fourth grade, what was going on in the world and lots of other stuff.

Some teachers go home as soon as the end-of-school bell rings. But Mrs. Mazursky stays late every day, talking with kids and helping kids who are having trouble reading or learning to multiply. She doesn't *make* anyone stay after school.

But everyone knows she'll help them if they want to stay.

Once, it was the Friday before Mother's Day, and I hadn't finished the Mother's Day pin we were making in art. Mrs. Mazursky stayed until four o'clock to help me finish my pin. I told you she was terrific!

The day I was kicked out of class, Mrs. Mazursky could tell right away there was something wrong.

"What's the matter, Stella?" she asked. "You look as if your cat, your dog and your pet canary were all run over by a truck. But I know you don't have any pets."

Usually, I would have laughed at Mrs. Mazursky's joke. But I just asked, "Can I talk to you alone?"

"Of course," said Mrs. Mazursky.

She told this kid, Paul, that he should keep practicing his handwriting and she would be back in a minute. Then she led me over to her desk and asked me what was wrong.

I told her about Rashoon's lying and then kicking me out of class and all. "You would never act like that," I said to her.

"Well . . ." she said.

"Isn't Mrs. Rashoon horrible?" I asked. I was careful to say *Mrs.* Rashoon, instead of just Rashoon.

"I really don't want to talk about another teacher," said Mrs. Mazursky.

"Yeah, I guess not," I said. "You believe my side of the story, though, don't you?"

"Yes," said Mrs. Mazursky. And she put her arm around me. At least, she still wanted to be my friend.

At home, I told my mother what happened in school. "I can't believe she lied like that!" I said. "And teachers are always telling kids not to lie."

"Don't take these things so seriously," said my mother. "Mrs. Rashoon probably didn't know what to say when she saw you at that table, so she said the first thing that came into her head."

"Well, how would you feel if you got kicked out of class?" I asked my mother. I started to cry when I thought of Rashoon barking at Ronnie just for talking to me.

"Oh, don't cry, Stella honey," said my mother, hugging me. "It's not so bad, is it? You feel better now, don't you? Don't you, Stella?"

"Yes," I said. But I didn't. My mother gets upset when I'm upset. She always wants me to say I feel fine, even when I don't. She ends up making me feel bad about feeling bad, if you know what I mean.

When Tom came home, I wanted to talk to him about Rashoon. I wanted to ask him if he thought I was dumb for going to the blue table in back of the classroom in the first place. And I wanted to ask him if teachers in high school lied like that. But then I saw that Tom had trouble of his own.

Two of his old girlfriends, Cheryl and Roberta, were waiting on the front step for him. And they both looked pretty angry.

Tanya didn't have much advice to offer other than "Da dee dee noo noo."

When my father came out of his office, I said, "Dad, can I talk to you about Rashoon?"

"Rashoon?" he said. "You mean that new TV computer game you've been asking me to get you for your birthday?"

"Never mind, Dad, forget it," I said.

"Don't give up so easily," he said. "If it's not too expensive, I'll consider it. You know, if it's 99¢ or under," he said, winking at me and thinking he was the funniest man in the world.

After a couple of days, I didn't feel as bad about Rashoon. I decided she was just an unpleasant fact of life, like the flu and broccoli and Monday morning. I promised myself to have as little to do with her as possible. Not every teacher could be perfect, like Mrs. Mazursky.

Chapter 6

"Guess who's coming for dinner tonight!" my mother said to me one spring afternoon.

"Tom's girlfriend," I said.

"Guess again," said my mother.

"Two of Tom's girlfriends," I said.

"It's a friend of *yours*," said my mother.

"Rachel? Debbie?" I said. "You didn't invite both of them, I hope!"

"It's neither of them," said my mother.

"Let me think . . . a friend of mine," I said. "Not Rachel, not Debbie . . . Is it a girl or a boy?"

"Neither," said my mother.

"What is it . . . a carrot?" I said.

"I'll give you a hint," said my mother. "It's a woman."

"A woman who's a friend of mine?" I said. "Mrs. Mazursky?"

"Yes!" said my mother.

"You should have told me before!" I said. "I have to find something nice to wear. I have to clean up my room. . . . I have to . . ."

"Take it easy," said my mother. "The reason I didn't tell you sooner is that I just ran into her at Bill's Foodmaster while you were playing outside. She mentioned that her husband is on a business trip. And I know both her kids are away at college. So I invited her for dinner."

"Well, I want to make sure everything's perfect," I said. And I ran off to clean my room.

I wanted Mrs. Mazursky to really like my house and my family. I hoped my father wouldn't say anything embarrassing, like calling her Mrs. Rashoon or something. And I hoped my mother wouldn't serve something horrible that she got on sale, like *liver*.

I picked up all my toys and clothes and threw them into my closet. It was so crowded in there that I had to lean against the door to make it close. I straightened my bed and ran downstairs to check on my mother in the kitchen.

It smelled really good in there. That was a hopeful sign. "What are you making?" I asked.

"Spaghetti sauce," she said.

My mother's spaghetti sauce is delicious. "Are you making spaghetti too?" I asked.

"No," said my mother. "I thought I'd serve the sauce on ice cream."

"You're kidding!" I said.

"Of course I'm kidding," said my mother. "Will you try to relax?"

"I can't, Mammu," I said. "I want Mrs. Mazursky to have a good time with us."

"Don't worry, she'll have a good time," said my mother.

"Goo time, goo time," said Tanya, who was playing with fruit-shaped magnets on the refrigerator. Tanya was actually starting to make sense. I got a kick out of her trying to say words. Sometimes you could almost have a real conversation with her. I hoped she wouldn't have a tantrum during dinner about something dumb, like wanting to play with the saltshaker and pour salt on her head.

"We'll sweep Mrs. Mazursky off her feet," my mother said to me. She picked me up and whirled me around until I started laughing.

I went back upstairs and put on a new blue dress with a white collar. I had never worn it before. Then I untied my braids and rebraided them as neatly as I could.

I was the first one at the door when Mrs. Mazursky rang the bell. She looked nice and friendly, as usual.

"Can I take your coat?" I asked her.

"That's very nice of you, Stella," she said. "But I'm not wearing a coat."

"Oh," I said, feeling my face turn as red as Elsie Hoover's when she gives a wrong answer.

"It was such a short walk from the driveway that I decided to leave my coat in the car," said Mrs. Mazursky.

Tom came running in. He had been playing football. I wished he didn't look so grubby. "Oh, hi, you're Stella's ex-teach, right?" said Tom.

"And you must be Tom," said Mrs. Mazursky.

"That's right," said Tom. "Hey Stella, how come you're wearing a dress? What's the big occasion?"

I didn't know what to say. I could feel myself getting redder.

"You look very nice, Stella," said Mrs. Mazursky.

Tom said he had to go change his clothes. I hoped he wouldn't say anything fresh during dinner.

"Rose, I'm so glad you could come," said my mother as she came into the hall, where Mrs. Mazursky and I were standing. I wished my mother didn't call her by her first name. She should call her Mrs. Mazursky.

Mrs. Mazursky didn't seem to mind though. "It was awfully nice of you to invite me, Rhoda," she said.

Tanya came running around the corner, pulling a toy dog on a string.

44

"Oh, she's adorable," said Mrs. Mazursky. "Stella's told me so much about her little sister!" She kneeled down to say "Hi" to Tanya. Just then, I smelled something awful.

"Doodoo!" said Tanya.

"I think you're right, Tanya," said Mrs. Mazursky, getting back on her feet quickly.

I thought I would die. My little sister had a great sense of timing.

My mother went off to change Tanya's diaper, and Mrs. Mazursky asked me for a tour of the house. I showed her the living room, the dining room and the kitchen. I knew I should have pointed out interesting things, but I was so nervous that all I could think of to say was, "This is the living room" or "This is the kitchen— We eat here."

As Mrs. Mazursky was looking at Tom's football trophies in the den, my father showed up. "Well, hello, Mrs. Mazursky," he said. I was glad he remembered her name.

"Hi, Mr. Nash," said Mrs. Mazursky. "Stella has been showing me your home. It's just lovely."

I had never thought of our house as lovely before, but I supposed it wasn't bad.

My mother came back into the living room with Tanya and said, "Dinner's ready." We all went into the kitchen.

My mother didn't burn the spaghetti or anything, and the sauce was delicious. Everybody said so, including Mrs. Mazursky. Even Tanya said so in her own way, by eating three helpings. She was very well-behaved and cute. She kept waving at Mrs. Mazursky and saying "Hi."

My father told a story about a client of his who was supposed to give a speech at a business meeting. When he took out his notes for the speech, it turned out he had his wife's shopping list instead.

Everybody laughed at my father's story.

"Your client sounds as absentminded as you," my mother said to my father. I hoped she wouldn't start criticizing him in front of Mrs. Mazursky.

I was so busy being nervous and hoping that no one would say anything dumb that *I* couldn't think of anything to say.

Suddenly, my mother said to me, "I hope that dress is washable."

I looked down and there, in the middle of my white collar, was a bright red spaghetti sauce stain. I felt like a jerk! I was more of a slob than Tanya.

"Oh well," said Mrs. Mazursky. "I'm sure it will wash out."

I didn't say anything. I was sure Mrs. Mazursky had decided I was a real loser. Not only was I boring—I didn't say a word all through dinner—but I was a slob too. I should never have worn a white collar when we were having spaghetti!

After dinner, Mrs. Mazursky offered to help clean up the kitchen. But my mother said, "No,

thanks." She said I should take Mrs. Mazursky on a tour of the upstairs rooms. It was nice to get out of having to help clean up after dinner for a change.

I showed Mrs. Mazursky my parents' room and Tanya's room. I didn't show her Tom's room because he was talking on the phone in there to Robin, his latest girlfriend.

Then I showed Mrs. Mazursky my room. She admired the rainbow-pattern curtains and bedspread my mother had made.

"Your room is so neat," she said. "When my kids were your age, you could hardly walk in their rooms, with all the toys on the floor."

Well, at least she thinks my room is neat, I thought. *Even if I'm boring and eat like a slob.*

Just then, Tom came in. "Stell, did I lend you my tape recorder?" he asked. "I need it in school tomorrow—let me look in your closet . . ."

"Tom, wait . . ." I started to say.

But it was too late. He opened my closet door, and 14,000 dolls, games, puzzles and books came flying out.

Now Mrs. Mazursky knows I'm sneaky too, I thought.

I had been so worried about my family acting dumb—about my father being forgetful and my mother cooking something creepy and Tanya having a tantrum and Tom being fresh. *They* had all acted great. *I* was the one who had acted as if I had the personality of a hermit crab and had got-

48

ten spaghetti sauce on my collar and then had half my room come flying out of my closet.

Tom waded through the pile of toys and books that were all over my floor, and he found the tape recorder. "Thanks," he said and left.

I waited to see if Mrs. Mazursky would say something like, "Ahem, young lady! So this is how you straighten a room—by stuffing everything into your closet?"

Instead, she looked at the mess on the floor and started roaring with laughter.

After a while, I started laughing too. I supposed it was pretty funny. Especially since my favorite doll, Alexandra, was lying on top of the mess with a big smile on her face.

"You're just like my kids after all," said Mrs. Mazursky, with as big a smile as Alexandra's.

We walked back downstairs, and Mrs. Mazursky said she had to be going. Everybody in my family said good-bye to her at the door.

"Well, it's been a very nice evening," she said. "It's great to get to know Stella's family. Stella has always been one of my favorite students. She's so bright and witty and eager to learn. I've missed having her in class this year."

Me? I thought. *Bright, witty, one of her favorite students?* Mrs. Mazursky didn't think I was a loser after all. She seemed to like me as much as I liked her!

I finally stopped being nervous. "See you in jail tomorrow," I said to my friend, Mrs. Mazursky.

49

Chapter 7

A couple of weeks after Mrs. Mazursky was over for dinner, I came home from school and found my mother cutting coupons out of the newspaper. She already had a big pile in front of her, and she was searching through the paper for more.

I noticed a 15¢-off coupon for a hot chocolate mix.

"We all hated this stuff the last time you bought it," I said. "It tasted like hot mud."

"The coupon says New and Improved!" said my mother.

"They always say that," I said. "They couldn't say Not Quite As Disgusting As It Used To Be, could they?"

"Oh, you're right," said my mother, tearing up the coupon. "You're fresh, but you're right. It's just that I'm upset, and it makes me feel better to clip coupons."

Some people cry or yell when they're upset. Or they go out and jog. My mother clips coupons.

"Why are you upset?" I asked.

"I got a little carried away today," she said. "There was a sale on refrigerators at the Crafton Appliance Center. One refrigerator was the prettiest shade of yellow, and Tanya kept pointing at it from her stroller and saying 'Pretty, pretty,' and it was marked 25 percent off and . . ."

"Mammu, you didn't," I said. She had bought a new refrigerator two months before.

"Wrong," said my mother. "I did."

"But we don't need a new refrigerator," I said.

"Don't remind me," said my mother. She looked as if she would either cry or kick the new yellow kitchen table she had bought on sale a couple of weeks before.

"When will it be delivered?" I asked.

"In two weeks," said my mother.

"Why don't you call up the store and cancel your order?" I asked.

"That's the problem," said my mother. "The sign said All Sales Final."

"Oh," I said.

"Daddy will be so angry," said my mother. "I promised him I would try not to be such a sale nut."

"Tell him you needed more room to put all the 59¢-a-pound chickens," I said, trying to make my mother laugh.

"Don't make jokes!" she said. "This is serious!"

It didn't seem fair that my mother was allowed to be upset, but whenever I was upset, she told me there was nothing to worry about. She looked so sad though, I had to feel sorry for her.

"We'll think of something, Mammu," I said. I suggested that she put an ad in the paper to sell the new refrigerator, or the old one, or one of them anyway. But she said you never get much money for secondhand appliances, even if they're hardly used. And she said my father would go nuts when he saw the refrigerator on their credit card bill.

Then I told her she could plead with the owner of the Crafton Appliance Center to take the refrigerator back. She could say she had a high fever when she bought it, and she didn't know what she was doing.

"The sign said All Sales Final—Absolutely No Exceptions," said my mother. "There's no way they would take it back."

"No way, man," said Tanya.

I started to laugh. "She's been hanging around with Tom," I said.

"Tom," said Tanya, grinning.

"Never mind," said my mother. "Let's get back to my refrigerator problem."

"Maybe you could tell Daddy you won the refrigerator in a contest," I said. "You're always entering contests."

My mother started to get excited about that idea. But then she said, "That won't work either. He would still see the refrigerator on our credit card bill."

There was no doubt about it. Mammu was in big trouble.

Chapter 8

I kept trying to think of ways to help my mother, the sale nut. We had only two weeks before the refrigerator would be delivered.

But then something exciting happened in school for a change. And I forgot all about my mother's problem.

Rashoon announced that the third and fourth grades would be having a softball tournament. Not only did it sound like fun, but whenever our class was in a game, we wouldn't have to wait for the three o'clock bell to get out of the classroom. We would play at two o'clock and then go straight home after the game. That meant we would get out of jail a whole hour early!

Our class's team turned out to be really good. Michael Brown and Ronnie Brazelton are excellent hitters. Debbie is a really fast runner and Elsie, the blushing giant, is not a bad pitcher.

I got picked to play center field. I'm not too hot at sports. So I asked my brother to give me some pointers. Tom spent a couple of afternoons hitting me high pops and line drives in a field near our house.

"Just don't freak out when the ball comes to you," he said. "Say to yourself, 'Hey, I can catch it, no sweat!' "

There were too many kids in our class for everyone to play in the field at the same time. So we took turns.

When it wasn't my turn in the field or when our class was up at bat, I had to switch between sitting next to Rachel and Debbie. They wouldn't get near each other.

Rachel hates sports. She said she would much rather be reading, or writing poetry than trying to hit a crummy little ball with a skinny bat.

I like to play sports sometimes, but not as often as we did in the tournament. Sitting on the bench is the best (and safest) position, as far as I'm concerned. Don't tell Tom, but I'm still afraid of the ball when it's coming at me at 2,000 miles per hour, even if I'm telling myself, "Hey, I can catch it, no sweat!"

When I told Debbie that I wasn't crazy about sports, she said, "You sound like your creepy friend, Rachel. Look at her over there, reading a book instead of cheering for our team."

When I told Rachel I thought the tournament was fun, she said, "You've been spending too much time with Debbie. She likes sports because she likes to win win win! And more than winning, she likes to see other people lose."

During the first game, Johnny Surbeck was catcher. He was running after a foul ball when he tripped on a rock and sprained his ankle.

"Poor guy," I said to Rachel. "He tried so hard to make that catch."

"It's silly to get hurt in sports," said Rachel. "Why should he hurt himself trying to win a dumb softball game?" Then she went back to reading *The History of Our Nation*. What fourth grader wastes her time reading *The History of Our Nation*? Especially during a softball game!

Later, I was sitting with Debbie. She was on the edge of her seat, rooting for our team. "That Johnny Surbeck is so clumsy," she said. "He never should have sprained his ankle." Debbie can be a little hardhearted at times.

Both Debbie and Rachel are a little hard*headed* most of the time. And *I* must be *soft*headed for trying to be friends with both of them.

In order to make the tournament fair, third grade teams got three runs added to their scores at the beginning of the game, whenever they played fourth grade teams.

Our class won our first four games easily. Then we won our fifth game 10–9. Suddenly, we were in the finals! We were playing Mrs. Mazursky's class for the championship. The winning class would get a trophy. And a framed photograph of the class, along with the trophy, would go in the display case next to the principal's office.

Everybody in my class, except Rachel, was excited about the final softball game. Debbie got her father to supply the class with T-shirts from one of his sporting goods stores. They were red with white letters. They said WINNERS!

For someone who wasn't crazy about sports, I was really hopped-up about the final game. I wanted our class to win, and *I* wanted to be good too.

I got Tom to cancel a date with Robin to give me a last-minute fielding lesson.

"You're getting pretty decent at catching," he said on our way home.

"Do you think Mrs. Mazursky will think I'm good?" I asked him.

"Sure," he said. "She'll wish you were on *her* team."

Mrs. Mazursky's class was excited about the tournament too. Even though they were only third graders, they were really good. And they had the advantage of having an enthusiastic teacher. You should have seen Mrs. Mazursky. She wore a baseball cap to all the games, and she paced up and down, cheering her class on.

You wouldn't want to see Rashoon. She just sat on the bench like a wart on a frog. You could tell she would rather be doing something else, like yelling at some poor student or giving our class more multiplication problems. When our class scored a run, she would raise one of her painted-on eyebrows and clap politely.

When Mrs. Mazursky's class scored, Mrs. Mazursky practically did a cartwheel. I kept wishing I had her for a teacher again.

In the big final game, our class started out "hot." We had a bunch of hits in the first three innings, and by the fourth inning, we were ahead 7–4, even with the three extra runs Mrs. Mazursky's class got added to their score because they were third graders, and we were fourth graders. When it was my turn in the field, I caught two balls and missed one.

Mrs. Mazursky really egged her team on and called lots of time-outs, so she could have conferences with the pitcher. I thought her spirit was terrific.

"Come on, let's earn that trophy!" she shouted. "Let's hit that ball out of here!"

After a while, I saw an expression on her face that told me she wasn't just trying to be nice to her team. She really took the game seriously. She wanted her class to win as much as they did, maybe more than they did.

In the fifth inning, when we were still ahead by three runs, Mrs. Mazursky started to do more than cheer for her team. She started to root against our team.

"Miss! Miss!" she shouted when our team was up at bat. I didn't think that was very sportsmanlike or sportswomanlike or however you say it. Tom always told me you're supposed to cheer for your team, not try to jinx the other team.

Mrs. Mazursky's class really went to town with their jeers, once they heard their teacher rooting against our team. "You can't pitch, you can't pitch!" they shouted when our team was in the field. When we were at bat, they yelled, "Easy out! The batter can't hit!"

I started feeling weird that Mrs. Mazursky was acting mean to our team. It was the first time she did something I didn't like.

I don't know if all the shouting helped Mrs. Mazursky's team, but they really started to hit the ball in the sixth inning. We had a nice three-run lead and then suddenly, they got a bunch of hits and we were only ahead 11 to 10.

We tried to get a bigger lead at the beginning of the seventh (the last) inning, but all our hitters struck out or popped out. It didn't help that Mrs. Mazursky started a cheer that went, "You're older. But we're better. You're bigger. But we're stronger." We felt creepy that a bunch of little third graders were giving us such a hard time.

When we made the third out in our half of the seventh inning, and the score was still 11 to 10, I thought Debbie would have a heart attack. She kicked the bench in anger. That hurt her toe, which made her even more angry. She hopped up and down like a crazy person. I almost started to laugh. But I didn't want to be next on her kicking list.

It was my turn to play center field in the last half of the inning. If Mrs. Mazursky's class didn't score any runs, our class would win. If they scored one run, the game would be tied, and it would go into extra innings. If they scored two runs, they would win the game and the tournament. They would get the trophy and their picture in the display case.

I told myself that if the ball came within three miles of center field, I had to catch it. I was nervous that it would come near me and I would miss it, which happened once in the third inning. I slammed my fist into my fielding glove, the way the players did on Tom's baseball team.

Elsie was pitching, so I thought we had a pretty good chance. The first batter on Mrs. Mazursky's team came to the plate, and Elsie struck him out in three pitches. A huge cheer went up from our field. Even Rachel, who was playing first base, let out a couple of whoops.

The second batter was Lois Sorenson, a fast, skinny kid. She hit the ball way over Kevin Landers' head in right field. By the time Kevin picked up the ball and threw it to the infield, Lois was on base.

"That's the way, Lois!" shouted Mrs. Mazursky. Her voice was almost gone.

The next batter was a kid named Ryan. He hit a ball way up in the air and Sally Andrews, our second baseman, caught it.

Two outs! If we could get one more out, we would have the championship. I really wanted to win now. I wanted to teach Mrs. Mazursky that it didn't pay to be unsportsmanlike or unsportswomanlike.

"If it comes to you, catch it," I kept telling myself. "Stay alert!"

The next batter was Richie Black, a pretty good hitter. Since Mrs. Mazursky had already started the jinxing cheers, our team shouted, "Strike out! Strike out!" But we had no chance being heard over the MEGAPHONE (yes!) that Mrs. Mazursky suddenly pulled out of a canvas bag and shouted into: "Elsie can't pitch! Elsie can't pitch!"

Elsie, who was wearing orange shorts with her red and white team T-shirt, blushed even redder than usual. Then she pitched the ball, and Richie hit it just a little too hard for our third baseman to catch. Richie made it to first base, and Lois ran to second.

I didn't like that at all. Now that Mrs. Mazursky's team had a runner on second base, they could tie the game if they got another hit.

David Schneider, a good hitter, came up to bat. I told myself that I could have French fries every night for a week if I caught a ball. Elsie, who was probably trying not to listen to "Elsie can't pitch!" threw the ball, and David hit it way up in the air toward (where else?) center field . . . me.

The ball was hit so hard that it would end up way behind me if it hit the ground. I turned around and started running like crazy, which is what Tom told me to do if there was a hard-hit ball. I tried to believe the chant Tom taught me . . . "Hey, I can catch it, no sweat!" But it was hard not to panic when I knew the whole tournament depended on me.

If I caught the ball, the base runners couldn't score, according to rules of softball. But, if I missed it, Lois and Richie Black, and maybe even David Schneider, would make it home and score. And we would lose the game, the tournament, the trophy and the framed picture in the display case.

I ran as fast as I could, which probably isn't very fast, trying to keep the ball in sight over my shoulder. Lois, Richie and David were taking a chance that I wouldn't catch it— They were racing around the bases.

The ball was coming down now. I couldn't believe it! I had run perfectly. I was in just the right spot to make the catch.

I held my glove out and hoped hoped hoped I could catch it. I had never caught a ball that was hit so high. It was almost in my glove now.

Remember to put your other hand over the ball after you catch it, the way Tom taught you, I thought.

There it was, in my glove. I had caught it! It was wobbling, not all the way in the glove. I started to cover it with my right hand.

"Drop it, Stella!" shouted Mrs. Mazursky through her megaphone.

And I did.

Lois made it home before I could even pick up the ball. Richie crossed home plate before I could throw it to the infield. David scored too, before Sally Andrews could throw it to our catcher. The score was Mrs. Mazursky's team 13, our team 11.

I had lost the whole tournament.

Just like that.

Mrs. Mazursky's class was shouting, "We're number one!" and running around in a big hug.

I sat on the ground and cried.

Rachel, Michael Brown and Sally Andrews came over to me.

"Hey, you gave it your best shot," said Michael.

"Don't take it so hard," said Sally.

"It's just a game," said Rachel, putting her arm around me.

Even Rashoon came over and said, "Good try, Stella."

65

I didn't say anything. I knew if I tried to talk, I would cry even harder.

Everybody thought I was crying because I had lost the tournament. But that was only part of it. I felt bad that I had dropped the ball, but it had been a hard ball to catch. I thought it was pretty good that I had caught it in the first place.

The thing that really broke me up was the way Mrs. Mazursky had acted. It was bad enough that she rooted against our team. But then she shouted at me to drop the ball. She was supposed to be my *friend.* I thought she was *perfect!*

I never felt so awful in my life. I felt even worse than when my father picked up the wrong birthday cake for my birthday party last year. I leaned forward to blow out the candles and I saw, in pink whipped cream, Happy Birthday Harry. I felt really crummy then, but that was nothing compared to the way I felt after the tournament.

Chapter 9

I went right home after the game. But I may as well have been alone in a desert or in a rowboat in the middle of the ocean. I didn't want to talk to anyone. I was too sad to do anything. I didn't watch TV. I didn't eat. I didn't play with Tanya.

When I walked in the house, my mother asked me what I wanted for a snack. I usually have milk with graham crackers or grape jelly on toast.

"I don't want anything," I said, starting to go to my room.

"How about some jelly donuts?" asked my

mother. "I've got two dozen of them. They were on sale at Dot's Donuts."

"No, thank you," I said.

"How about some juice?" she asked, following me.

"No," I said.

"An apple?"

"No." If she had offered me French fries and a hot fudge sundae with whipped cream, I would have said "No" too.

"What's wrong?" asked my mother.

"Nothing," I said.

I wanted to go to my room and be miserable by myself. I didn't want my mother to keep asking me questions, because if she did, I would start to cry. Then I would end up telling her about the tournament and Mrs. Mazursky turning out to be a witch. I knew she would just say, "Oh, you don't really feel so bad, do you?" And I didn't need her telling me I didn't feel bad, when I felt plenty bad.

"How was the tournament?" she asked.

"We lost," I said.

"So that's it," she said.

I didn't say anything. I went to my room and closed the door.

I was just about to have a good cry when there was a knock on the door. Tom stuck his head in.

"Stell baby, Mom says your team lost," he said.

"Yeah," I said.

"How was your fielding?" he asked.

"I dropped the ball and lost the game," I said.

"Oh," he said. "I know how you must feel."

"No, you don't," I said. He didn't know how Mrs. Used-To-Be-Perfect Mazursky had acted. But I didn't feel like telling him about her. I felt embarrassed to have thought a teacher was perfect. Also, Tom would never understand my troubles because everything is easy for him. He does great in school, he makes all the sports teams, and he has more girlfriends than he knows what to do with.

"Did you make any catches?" asked Tom.

"Yes," I said. "I made two outs. And the ball I dropped at the end was hit really hard. I had to run a long way to catch it."

"Tough break," said Tom.

"Listen, Tom, I don't feel like talking," I said.

"Hey, that's cool," said Tom. "I don't want to step on your space or anything."

And he backed out the door.

Ten minutes later, my father shouted through the door, "Stell, can I come in?"

I wiped my eyes and pretended to be putting stickers in my sticker album. "Sure, come in," I said.

"I hear you're a little down in the dumps," he said. "Want to talk?"

"No," I said. Even if I wanted to talk to him, he probably wouldn't remember who Mrs. Mazursky was. And he would never admit that he forgot anything.

Since I wouldn't talk, he tried to make me laugh. He started talking in a phony English accent that usually cracks me up. But it didn't work this time. Then he made funny faces. He stuck out his tongue, crossed his eyes, wiggled his ears, puffed out his cheeks, waved his arms and walked like a bird. That didn't work either. I just stared at him. Finally, he gave up and left.

I kept to myself the rest of the weekend. Debbie and Rachel phoned about three times each, but I told my mother to say I was asleep or in the bath or in another galaxy.

On Sunday night, I was feeling even more down, if that's possible, because I knew I had to go to school the next day. I considered running away or pretending I was sick, so I wouldn't have to see my friends or my former friend, Mrs. Mazursky.

After dinner, I got into a warm bubble bath and tried to decide what to do.

My mother opened the door and said, "I want to talk to you."

"I'm sorry, Mom, I haven't come up with any good ideas for getting rid of the extra refrigerator," I said.

"It's not about the refrigerator," she said. "I'd like to know what's bothering you."

"Nothing," I said. "What makes you think something is bothering me?"

"When her daughter doesn't say more than six words to her in two days, a mother starts to wonder what's wrong," she said. "I know it's not just the softball tournament. You don't care that much about sports."

"OK, you win," I said. "Something else is bothering me."

"Now we're getting somewhere," said my mother.

"But I don't feel like talking about it," I said. And I gave my rubber duck a push that made him swim the whole length of the bathtub.

"Now we're *not* getting anywhere," said my mother. She gave me a what-am-I-going-to-do-with-you look and then said, "Let me put it this way . . . I'm not leaving this bathroom until you tell me what's going on with you."

There seemed to be no way out unless I drowned in the bath water or stayed in the tub until I caught pneumonia and had to be rushed to Crafton General Hospital. Neither drowning nor pneumonia appealed to me. So I took a deep breath and told my mother how I used to be crazy about Mrs. Mazursky, and how she turned out to be a real meanie, even jinxing me to drop the ball.

"It's like when I found out there was no Santa Claus, only worse," I told my mother. "Mrs. Mazursky was like Santa Claus, Wonder Woman, the Easter Bunny, and the president of the United States all rolled into one."

I waited for my mother to tell me I really didn't

feel so bad, as if she knew what was going on in my head better than I did.

Instead, she said, "Oh, how sad, Stella! You must feel awful!"

"I used to think Mrs. Mazursky was perfect!" I said. And I started to cry. "She's perfect all right, perfectly horrible," I said between sobs.

My mother helped me out of the bathtub. She gave me a big hug. "It sounds like Mrs. Mazursky got carried away during the game," said my mother. "She's really a fine teacher and a fine woman. She probably wanted her class to win so badly that she didn't realize what she was doing."

"Well, she ought to know what she's doing," I said. "She's a teacher."

"*She* probably feels bad about what she did too," said my mother.

"I'll never forgive her," I said.

"I can understand your being angry with her," said my mother. "Hey, you're getting me all wet!" she said. She started to laugh. "Here I am hugging you, and I forgot you're not dry yet."

I started to laugh too when I saw big wet splotches all over the new blouse she had bought on sale at Bermans Department Store.

I put on my robe and went into the living room with my mother. My father was entertaining Tanya. He was crawling around on the floor with her on his back. "Neigh neigh!" she shouted.

My father looked exhausted after taking care of

Tanya for the ten minutes or so my mother had been in the bathroom with me.

"Now I see why you don't want to get a job," he said to my mother. "Looking after Tanya is a full-time job alone. And you've got Stella and Tom to take care of too."

"And you!" said my mother.

"Mommy! Mommy!" said Tanya. "Book!"

"OK," said my mother. "We'll read one book, and then it's night-night time. Stella, why don't you tell Daddy what you just told me?"

So I did.

Surprisingly enough, my father really listened. His mind didn't seem to be in another galaxy, as usual.

"You know," he said, "I had something like that happen to *me* when I was a kid."

"Really?" I asked.

"Yes," said my father. "It wasn't a teacher who disappointed me. It was my friend's father. He was terrific . . . an excellent athlete, a well-known lawyer, had a great sense of humor. He used to take us to ball games and the movies. I was crazy about him."

My father sighed and started getting his usual faraway look.

"Dad?" I said.

He didn't answer.

"Dad?" I repeated. "What happened to your friend's father?"

"Oh," he said. "He promised to take us on a

camping trip one time. I was really excited. I had never been camping before. My friend and I spent days getting ready for the trip. Then, at the last minute—we were all packed and everything—his father canceled out. He said he had an important meeting with a client. I was so disappointed in him, I thought I would never speak to him again."

"Did you?" I asked.

"Not for a couple of months," he said. "But then I realized that, well, no one is perfect. *You* have to learn that too, Stella. And so does Tom. Every time he finds one thing wrong with one of his girlfriends, he drops her. Pretty soon, he'll probably drop Anita too, and she's a nice girl."

"You mean Robin, Dad," I said.

"Right, Robin," said my father. "You see, I told you no one's perfect. You may have noticed, for instance, that I'm a little absentminded at times."

I had to laugh at that comment. I had never heard my father admit he was absentminded before. Suddenly, I realized I felt much better. At least, my parents seemed to understand how disappointed I was in Mrs. Mazursky. I was glad I had decided to talk to them instead of drowning in the bathtub or catching pneumonia from staying in the bath all night.

Chapter 10

The next day in school, Debbie, Rachel and Michael Brown asked me why I hadn't returned their phone calls. I didn't feel like telling them I had spent the weekend sulking in my room. So I said I was busy. It was true— I was busy being miserable.

I didn't expect to be the most popular person in Rashoon's class after making us lose the softball tournament. So it surprised me when at least six kids, including Ms. Win-Win-Win Debbie, said they thought I had made a great try to catch that last ball.

"If Mrs. Mazursky hadn't jinxed you, you would have held on to it," said Debbie.

"Maybe," I said.

Rashoon had us do the same old _____ (you can fill in the blank with a not-so-nice word) multiplication worksheets all morning. Usually, I would have passed notes to Debbie and muttered to Rachel about what a witch Rashoon was. But I didn't have the old "fighting spirit" left in me. Things didn't seem the same now that I knew Mrs. Mazursky was a regular person, with things about her I didn't like. I knew I wouldn't be chatting with her during lunch or stopping by to visit her after school. Not that day or any other day.

On the way to the lunchroom, we passed the display case next to the principal's office. There, in all its gold-plated, shining glory, was Mrs. Mazursky's class's trophy. I felt sick to see it.

There were grilled cheese and tomato sandwiches for lunch, which is one of the only decent things the cafeteria serves. But I could only eat a microbite. I kept picturing that trophy in the display case, and I wasn't hungry.

On my way to the window where you return the trays, Mrs. Mazursky stopped me. "Stella, may I talk to you?" she asked.

I wouldn't look at her. I dumped the seven-eighths of my grilled cheese and tomato sandwich into the garbage can.

"I feel terrible about shouting at you during the game," she said. "I guess I just . . ."

I threw my milk carton in the garbage can and walked away, leaving Mrs. Mazursky stranded in the middle of her apology. I didn't want to have anything to do with her.

During recess, Debbie started a game of follow-the-leader. I felt like playing about as much as I felt like playing center field in a softball game again. But Debbie made a big deal about how I should play. As usual, I went along with her, so she wouldn't drop me like a hot potato pancake. I figured I needed all the friends I could get, now that I didn't have Mrs. Mazursky for a friend.

Of course, Debbie was the leader. She always comes up with neat things to follow. First, she had us go down the slide. Then we had to run across the softball field, waving our arms like birds. After that, we had to recite "Humpty Dumpty" in a French accent. It was kind of fun. After a while, I started to have a good time.

We hopped up and down for a while. Then we shouted, "We're still number one!" We walked backwards with our eyes closed, and we did a dance called the Funky Fox.

Along the way, a couple of new kids joined the game. There were about twelve kids playing when we passed Rachel reading a book on a swing.

"Hey, Rachel, want to play?" Lucy Talbot shouted.

"No!" said Debbie. "She can't play!"

"Why not?" asked Lucy.

"Because I'm the leader, and I said so," said Debbie, stamping her feet so her blonde curls bounced too.

"Come on, Debbie . . ." I began.

"Anyone who wants Rachel to play can stay here with Rachel," said Debbie. Then she looked at me and said, "Anyone who wants to be *my* friend can follow me." And she ran to the jungle gym.

About six kids ran after her. The rest of us stared at them.

"I'd better go too," said Elsie, who was clenching two Tootsie Rolls in her hands. And she ran off, followed by Sally Andrews and Kevin Landers.

That left Michael Brown and me.

"Aren't you two going?" asked Rachel.

"Not me," said Michael.

"Me neither," I said.

I couldn't believe it was happening. Debbie was finally going to drop me. I was pretty sure she had started the whole follow-me-or-else trick to get me to give up Rachel. But I wasn't going to.

Suddenly, I felt relieved as anything. Ever since I had become friends with Debbie, I'd been afraid she would drop me. And now that I knew she would, I was happy about it. Debbie may be rich and popular and clever and pretty. And she may have the nicest clothes in our class. And being her friend may have helped me to be popular too. But she made me do things I didn't like.

I thought about the time we blackmailed Elsie and the time we hid Debbie's brother's homework. Suddenly, I realized I had some nerve being angry with Mrs. Mazursky for not being perfect. I was far from perfect myself.

I decided that even if Debbie didn't drop me, I would drop her. Like a hot French fry, right out of the deep fryer.

Maybe Rachel didn't look or act like most fourth graders, but she was a really nice person.

"Rachel," I said. "You're stuck with me."

"Me too," said Michael.

"You're worth more than two Debbies," I said. "Maybe even three. I haven't worked out the multiplication."

"Please don't mention math during recess," said Rachel with a smile.

Chapter 11

That night, I gave myself a really big homework assignment. I decided to try to become as close to perfect as I could.

I didn't want to make anyone feel bad again, the way Mrs. Mazursky had made me feel.

First, I wanted to make up for all the mean things I had done in the past. I wrote a letter to Elsie, apologizing for the time Debbie and I blackmailed her. Next, I wrote to Miss Simpson, the substitute, to say I was sorry for taking advantage of her.

Then I wrote a list of ways to improve myself:

1. Try to be nice to everyone, even creeps.
2. Tell Mammu dinner is terrific, even when it's yucko.
3. Laugh at Daddy's stories, even the ones he's told 43½ times.
4. Try not to stare at Tom's girlfriends' pimples.
5. Don't get impatient with Tanya when she wants to read the same book six times in a row. . . .

There was a knock on my door.

"Who is it?" I asked, hiding the list under my geranium plant. I promised myself to start singing softly to the plant every day, because I heard that plants like music.

"It's Daddy," said my father. He opened the door and said, "Come see the surprise your mother gave me."

He led me to his office. The rest of my family was already there, and so was a bright yellow refrigerator with a price tag from the Crafton Appliance Center.

"Your mother had a brainstorm to get a refrigerator for my office!" said my father. "It's a nuisance for me to have to walk through the house to get snacks and drinks for my clients. Now I have my own refrigerator in my office!"

"That's great, Dad," I said.

My mother winked at me.

"Fidge!" said Tanya, pointing at the refrigerator.

"Excellent color!" said Tom.

"It's really a nice present," said my father. "And it's not even my birthday. Is it?"

"Such a man I married!" said my mother. "He doesn't even remember when his birthday is."

"By the way, was this refrigerator on sale?" my father suddenly asked with a suspicious look in his eye.

My mother stared at the floor. "Well . . ." she said.

"You promised not to go chasing after sales anymore," said my father.

"No one's perfect, Dad," I said. "You told me so yourself."

"That's true," said my father. "But your mother told me . . ."

"At least I didn't buy a new stove or a dishwasher or a garbage disposal," said my mother. "They were all on sale too."

"I suppose that's progress," said my father.

We all laughed.

It's true, no one is perfect, I thought. *Not my family. Not my friends. Not me. Not even Mrs. Mazursky.*

I decided I might talk to Mrs. Mazursky again after all. At least, I would apologize to her for not letting her apologize to me. And then she could finish apologizing, and who knows, by that time, maybe we would be friends again.

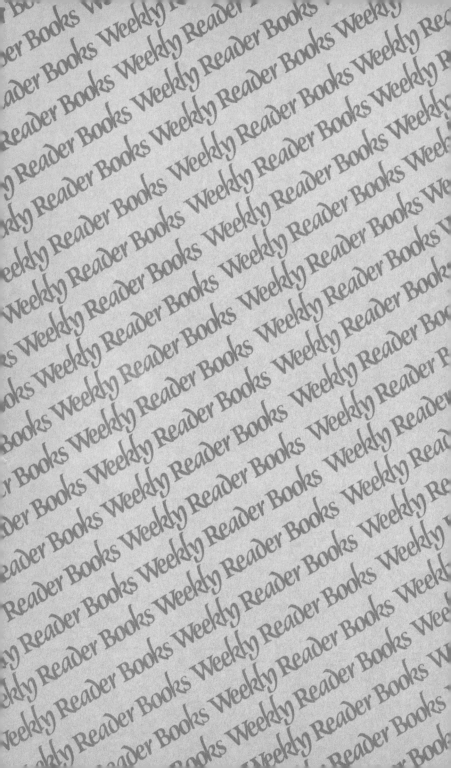